S0-ALL-729

Topic: Myself   **Subtopic:** Body Parts

Notes to Parents and Teachers:

It is an exciting time when a child begins to learn to read! Creating a positive, safe environment to practice reading is important to encourage children to love to read.

REMEMBER: PRAISE IS A GREAT MOTIVATOR!

Here are some praise points for beginning readers:

- You matched your finger to each word that you read!
- I like the way you used the picture to help you figure out that word.
- I love spending time with you listening to you read.

Book Ends for the Reader!

Here are some reminders before reading the text:

- Carefully point to each word to match the words you read to the printed words.

- Take a 'picture walk' through the book before reading it to notice details in the illustrations. Use the picture clues to help you figure out words in the story.

- Get your mouth ready to say the beginning sound of a word to help you figure out words in the story.

Words to Know Before You Read

ears

eyes

fingers

hands

head

mouth

nose

toes

MY GREAT BODY

By Carolyn Kisloski

Illustrated by
Nina de Polonia

rourkeeducationalmedia.com

Park County Library
P. O. Box 33
Guffey, CO 80820

I have one head.

I can wear a hat.

I have two eyes.

I can see my friends.

Hello!

I have two ears.

I can hear the birds.

Chirp!
Chirp!

Chirp!

I have one nose.

I can smell the flowers.

Sweet!

I have one mouth.

I can taste the ice cream.

Yummy!

13

I have two hands.

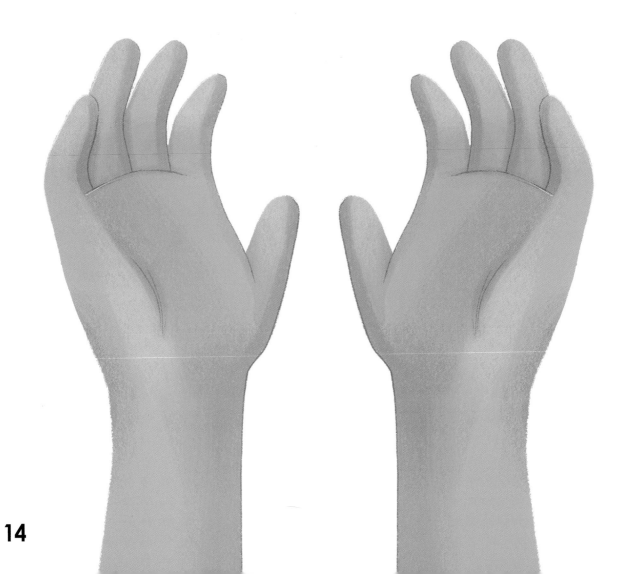

I can clap to music.

15

I have ten fingers.

I can feel my teddy bear.

17

I have two legs.

Boing!
Boing!
I can run and jump.

19

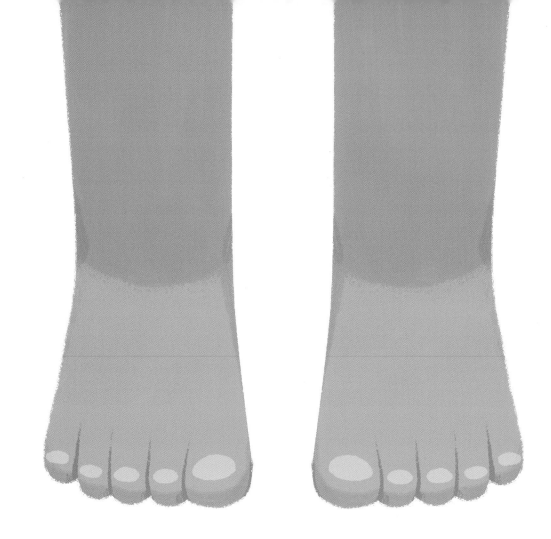

I have ten toes.

I can wiggle them.

Wiggle Wiggle

Book Ends for the Reader

I know...

1. What can you do with your eyes?

2. What can you do with your ears?

3. What can you do with your nose?

I think ...

1. What do you like to do with your hands?

2. What do like to do with your legs?

3. What is your favorite body part?

Book Ends for the Reader

What happened in this book?

Look at each picture and talk about what happened in the story.

About the Author

Carolyn Kisloski has been a life-long teacher, currently teaching kindergarten at Apalachin Elementary School, in Apalachin, NY. She is married and has three grown children. She enjoys spending time at the beach and the lake, playing games, and being with her family. Carolyn currently lives in Endicott, NY.

About the Illustrator

Nina de Polonia was born in the Philippines in 1985. She has loved drawing ever since she could hold a pencil. Aside from illustrating children's books, she's also a crocheter, calligrapher, herb gardener, and a full-time mom.

Library of Congress PCN Data

My Great Body / Carolyn Kisloski

ISBN 978-1-68342-700-1 (hard cover)(alk. paper)
ISBN 978-1-68342-752-0 (soft cover)
ISBN 978-1-68342-804-6 (e-Book)
Library of Congress Control Number: 2017935346

Rourke Educational Media
Printed in the United States of America, North Mankato, Minnesota

© 2018 Rourke Educational Media

All rights reserved. No part of this book may be reproduced or utilized in any form or by any means, electronic or mechanical including photocopying, recording, or by any information storage and retrieval system without permission in writing from the publisher.

www.rourkeeducationalmedia.com

Edited by: Debra Ankiel
Art direction and layout by: Rhea Magaro-Wallace
Cover and interior Illustrations by: Nina de Polonia